EARLY READER

Vedra & Krimon
Twin Beasts of Avantia

D0009292

Vedra & Krimon: Twin Beasts of Avantia was originally published as a Beast Quest special. This version has been specially adapted for developing readers.

With special thanks to Allan Frewin and
Fiona Munro

Reading Consultant: Prue Goodwin, lecturer in literacy and
children's books

ORCHARD BOOKS
An imprint of Hachette Children's Group
Part of the Watts Publishing Group
Carmelite House, 50 Victoria Embankment, London EC4Y 0DZ
Vedra & Krimon: Twin Beasts of Avantia first published in 2008 by Orchard Books
This Early Reader edition published in 2016
Text © Beast Quest Limited 2008, 2014
Cover illustrations © David Wyatt 2008; Beast Quest Limited 2014
Inside illustrations © Beast Quest Limited 2008, 2014

A CIP catalogue record for this book is available
from the British Library.

ISBN 978 1 40833 500 0

1 3 5 7 9 10 8 6 4 2

Printed in China

Orchard Books is a division of Hachette Children's Books,
an Hachette UK company.
www.hachette.co.uk
www.beastquest.co.uk

Vedra & Krimon
Twin Beasts of Avantia

BY ADAM BLADE

ORCHARD

STORY ONE

TWIN BEASTS

Welcome to the kingdom of Avantia, where magical Beasts protect the land. I am Aduro, a good wizard. Twin dragons, Vedra and Krimon, have been born and are in danger from the evil wizard Malvel. Our brave young heroes, Tom and Elenna, have helped before. Can they keep these Beasts safe from harm?

TWIN BEASTS

At the Royal Palace of Avantia a birthday party for King Hugo was taking place. As Tom and his friend Elenna raised their glasses in a toast, Elenna whispered in Tom's ear, "Here's to the six beasts of Avantia!"

"Shhh!" warned Tom. Most people believed the Beasts that protected the land were only a legend. But Tom and Elenna had seen them, and freed them from Malvel, an evil wizard.

The good wizard Aduro led the friends away from the party and spoke solemnly to them.

"Two new Beasts have been created," said Aduro. "They are twin dragons, and their names are Vedra and Krimon."

"Baby dragons!" gasped Elenna, excited. But Aduro was not smiling.

"Their birth could put Avantia in danger," he said, and conjured an image on the wall. It showed the two dragons sleeping in a dark cave. One was green and the other red. Tom and Elenna gazed at the dragons, enchanted.

"Vedra is green and Krimon red," began Aduro as the vision faded. "It is rare for two Beasts to be created together.

If Malvel hears about the twins,
he will use them for evil purposes
and harm Avantia. Will you help
to protect the dragons and stop
Malvel?"

"Of course we will!" promised
Tom and Elenna.

The wizard led Tom and
Elenna to a room with a huge
wooden chest in the middle.
Next to it lay Tom's shield and
sword, along with Elenna's bow
and a quiver of arrows.

Aduro climbed inside.
Puzzled, Tom followed, with his

sword and shield. His shield was decorated with powerful tokens from their previous Quests which would protect them. Elenna followed with her bow and arrows.

The bottom of the chest slid away to reveal a stairway down to a rushing river. A small rowing boat waited there.

"This is the hidden River Dour," Aduro said to Tom. "The river will take you to the dragons' cave. You and Elenna must go alone."

"Rocks!" Tom gasped
suddenly, as they fought to steer
the boat safely. Tom knew that
the splinter of Sepron's tooth in
his shield would protect them
from water, but not rocks!

Far ahead, they saw a faint
light, like a steady flame. It
grew stronger as the water

became calm and the little boat floated gently into a wide underground lake.

"Look!" gasped Tom, pointing. A large creature was swimming towards them.

"It's Sepron!" Elenna shouted joyfully. The huge sea serpent let out a cry of welcome.

Slowly, they became aware of the other Beasts. Stepping ashore, they saw Arcta the mountain giant peering down at them. The huge fire dragon, Ferno, stood nearby as Nanook the snow monster and Epos the flame bird welcomed them.

Clopping hooves announced the arrival of Tagus the horseman. He picked up Tom and Elenna and cantered away, followed by the other friendly Beasts.

After a short ride, Tagus stopped and they got down.

There were two newborn
dragons lying in a nest of
golden straw.

"We have to protect these
trusting beasts," Tom whispered
as Vedra began gently pecking
at Elenna's hair.

Tom pulled the magical map

from beneath his shirt. Aduro
had given it to him when he
began his very first Quest.
Unfolding the parchment, he
saw snow-covered mountains
rise up in sharp points. The
map was alive! A tiny light
showed where they had found
the dragons. A slender golden
path led northwards. It was
pointing the way to the snowy
land of Rion.

Elenna rushed to get the
food and the cloaks, while Tom
spoke to the baby dragons.

"I'm here to protect you," he began.

"*We* are here to protect them, you mean," said Elenna, returning with their things.

With a heavy flapping of wings, Ferno and Epos rose into the air, circling the cave. Ferno

carried Elenna and Vedra, while Tom and Krimon clung to Epos's back. Aduro's cloaks kept them warm as the great creatures flew north above the wintry landscape.

It was early afternoon when Tom saw high mountains ahead. He looked at the map, and a golden glow showed that they were close to Rion.

Then Tom noticed that one mountain was different from the others. It had a crater that glowed with a fierce red fire.

"It's a volcano!" Tom shouted.

Epos let out a croak of alarm as molten rock gushed up into the air. Tom saw Elenna and Vedra struggle to hold onto Ferno's back as he swerved to avoid the fountain of fire. He threw his shield up and the magical dragon scale on it saved them from the fiery rock, but as Ferno turned, Elenna's bow and arrows fell into the flaming crater.

Epos tried hard to pull back,

and Tom felt himself slipping.

"No!" he cried, falling from Epos's back and plunging helplessly downwards. A rushing sound filled his ears until, suddenly, Epos caught him with a triumphant shriek.

Exhausted and dazed, they flew on until the volcano was far behind them. At last Epos and Ferno landed on a remote slab of rock where, strangely, a boy was curled up as if asleep. As they approached, his eyes snapped open and he jumped to his feet.

"My name is Seth," he said, smiling and holding out his hand. But as Tom reached out his own hand, the boy lunged forwards, and threw him to the ground. Gasping for breath,

Tom saw that Seth had a
bronze sword in his hand, and it
was pointed at his throat.

Tom twisted to one side as
the sword struck the rock close
to his head. Seth stumbled
forwards and Tom jumped up.

Sparks flew as their swords
clashed again and again,
the noise echoing around
the mountain peaks that
surrounded them.

At last, Tom was able to kick
the blade out of Seth's grip,
and point his own sword at the
boy's neck.

"I'm sorry!" Seth gasped.

"I didn't mean to hurt you. I was half crazy with hunger and fear."

Tom picked up the bronze sword and slipped it into his own belt before allowing Seth to stand up.

Elenna gave Seth some bread to eat. The boy explained how he had become separated from his party while out hunting.

Tom and Elenna exchanged a wary look but Seth seemed so tired and frail they decided to give him another chance.

Spying a clearing, Elenna and Ferno swooped down, but as Epos prepared to follow, Tom saw Seth take a small leather pouch of golden powder from his jacket.

"The deadly magic of Malvel!" roared Seth, his eyes burning bright.

"No!" Tom shouted, as Seth leaned forward and hurled golden dust into Epos's eyes. The bird let out a deafening croak as Seth laughed, throwing more of the golden

dust into Tom's face. The powder
filled his eyes, stinging badly
and blinding him as Epos fell to
the ground and crash-landed.

Tom stumbled helplessly across the snowy ground, calling out for Elenna.

"Stay there," she said calmly when she had rushed over to him. "I'll get some water from the river for your eyes."

Tom listened to the noises of the frightened Beasts. A moment later, he felt icy water splash onto his face and cautiously opened his eyes.

There was a golden glow at the edges of Tom's vision but at least he could see again.

Seth and his bronze sword had both disappeared.

Back at the clearing, Epos was shaking her head from side to side, trying to clear the dust from her eyes. Krimon came creeping from where he had been hiding under Ferno's wing.

"Where has Vedra gone?" Elenna gasped, her eyes searching around desperately.

"Seth must have taken him," Tom replied, his voice full of anger and guilt.

A deep hollow laugh echoed across the treetops. It was the evil wizard, Malvel.

STORY TWO

DANGER IN RION

Hello again, my friends. Tom and Elenna's Quest is far from over! Malvel is close by and his servant, Seth, has stolen Vedra away. Both young dragons are in danger. There is much to do before the full moon rises tonight.

DANGER IN RION

Tom stared grimly into the howling blizzard. Epos was recovering from Seth's evil attack, but it would be a while before she could fly again. Ferno crawled closer to Epos, lifting one wing to protect her. Krimon had been huddled up against Ferno's side, but now he suddenly stood up and headed towards the forest.

"I think he can sense his

brother," Tom said. "Let's go
after him."

Tom and Elenna followed
Krimon. He snorted and
carried on, trotting deeper into
the dark forest.

Krimon paused and closed his eyes. A long bright flame streamed upwards from his nostrils and hung in the air, gradually changing into a bright fireball. At the same time, an orange glow was spreading over his leathery skin. Over his heart there shone a patch of emerald green light as strong as the fireball.

"What does it mean?" whispered Elenna.

"I think it shows the bond between the two baby dragons,"

Tom replied. "They're linked in some way."

Tom and Elenna followed Krimon as, with a snort, the dragon ran back into the wood.

"If Malvel puts his spell on the dragons when the moon is full, they will be evil for ever – and we won't be able to save them."

Suddenly, as if he understood, Krimon pushed his head into the hole Tom had made in the hedge. A burst of orange flame came pouring from the Beast's mouth.

"He's burning his way through!" exclaimed Elenna.

Tom and Elenna followed Krimon through the burnt gap in the hedge to the other side.

Before them were paths leading through rows of more holly bushes. But which path should they take?

The orange glow on Krimon's chest had become pale and the ball of fire in front of them was even dimmer. Tom knew this must mean Vedra was far away.

The Beast ran forward, trying out different paths until the light on his chest and the ball of flame brightened, meaning they were getting closer to Vedra.

Suddenly, Elenna gave a yelp of alarm as a flash of fire appeared in front of her. As they watched, more flashes appeared along the path.

"I don't like this," Elenna said. "These lights aren't here to help us. This is dark magic."

"Get back!" Tom shouted suddenly, leaping in front of

Elenna as a monstrous creature reared above them.

Tom raised his sword at the human-shaped monster. It was dark green, with long claws, sharp teeth and eyes that glowed red like boiling blood. It was a moment before Tom realised the creature wasn't moving.

"It's just a statue!" Tom said, turning to Elenna with a grin.

The hedges were filled with many similar hideous statues, all half hidden by holly.

The brave friends plunged onwards, until they came to two pathways exactly alike.

Krimon chose the right-hand path. Tom and Elenna followed, but straight away they were surrounded by a swirling green mist. Tom began to feel a terrible pain in his head and closed his eyes. When he opened them again, Malvel was standing there.

With a cry of rage Tom ran towards the evil wizard, his sword raised.

"I have to fight him!" he shouted to Elenna.

"There's no one there!" she gasped. "The headache and the mist are making you see things."

Tom, Elenna and Krimon trudged through the snow until they reached a wide chasm. While Tom and Elenna wondered how they would ever get across, Krimon spread his wings and took a giant leap, then landed safely on the far side.

Thinking fast, Tom cut a branch from the hedge and sliced off the smaller twigs until he had made a smooth pole twice his own height. As Elenna watched in amazement, Tom took a deep breath and then ran forward. The pole hit the ground and Tom sprang into the air and over the gap, landing safely beside Krimon. He threw the pole back to Elenna and soon she was standing beside him.

Continuing along the snowy path, Tom noticed that Krimon began to whine as if in pain. Finally, he fell to the ground.

"What's happening?" Elenna asked, trying to comfort him.

Tom sank to his knees beside the dragon, feeling panic rising. "Something bad must be happening to Vedra. Krimon is suffering the same pain!"

Suddenly the fireball over Krimon's head went out, and the orange and green glow on his chest disappeared.

"The link between Vedra and Krimon has been broken," Tom said sadly. "Something very bad must have happened."

Without the dragon to guide them, how would they get to the heart of the maze?

"What are we going to do now?" Elenna asked, tears shining in her eyes.

Tom racked his brains for an answer but Malvel's evil magic was playing tricks on his mind again. Then he heard a dragon whimpering.

"Be quiet!" Tom shouted at Krimon.

"Tom!" Elenna frowned. "He isn't making a sound."

Tom looked at Krimon. Elenna was right.

"It's Vedra!" he said, suddenly

realising where the sound came from.

"What do you mean? I can't hear anything," Elenna said.

"He's this way!" Tom said, running down the path. Elenna and Krimon followed behind.

Then she stooped to snatch the
bronze sword from Seth's fingers.

"Go and help Krimon!" she
called, throwing Tom the sword.

Watching the dragons fight
was terrifying. The moon was

high in the sky and time was
running out. Tom remembered
Aduro's words. He had to touch
Vedra's underbelly with the tip
of his sword. He ran in close but
his sword struck Vedra's foreleg.

The metal rang uselessly against the dragon's hard scales.

Tom stared at the silver moon and a plan formed in his mind. He tilted his sword so that its blade caught the moon's reflection. A flash of light struck

Vedra in the eyes. Dazzled and
blinded, the Beast reared up and
Tom sprang forward to touch his
belly with the sword.

Tom stood firm, blinded by
a sudden wind that swept over
them. Slowly he opened his eyes.

Vedra and Krimon were beside
him. Elenna was nearby, but
Seth and the bronze sword were
gone.

"We did it!" Tom said with
a grin. The dragons were

recovering. Vedra was safe from harm, cured of Malvel's evil.

Tom brought the magic map out of his tunic and unrolled it. "We're in the middle of nowhere!" he groaned.

"Look!" said Elenna, pointing into the sky. Their friends Ferno and Epos were winging their way towards them over the snowy forest.

When Ferno and Epos landed, the twins clambered onto Ferno's back and the great dragon took to the skies again.

They flew away towards Rion.
Tom and Elenna climbed
onto Epos's back. Tom looked
again at the map, and a
shimmering face appeared. It
was Aduro the wizard.

"Thanks to you, the twin dragons will grow up in a place of safety," he explained. "Ferno will stay by their side to teach and protect them."

Epos launched herself into the night sky, and sped southwards. Tom had succeeded in his quest and the twin Beasts of Avantia were safe. Now they could go home.

Home to Avantia.

If you enjoyed this story, you may want to read

Kragos and Kildor
The Two-Headed Demon
EARLY READER

Here's how the story begins...

Tom thundered along on his black stallion, Storm, with his friend Elenna behind him. Tom's father, Taladon, rode beside him across the green hills of Avantia. Taladon had been imprisoned by an evil sorcerer, Malvel. He had finally escaped when Tom weakened Malvel's magic. But Taladon had existed only as a ghost until Tom found the six pieces of the Amulet of Avantia. In the struggle for the final piece, Tom had wounded Malvel and banished him from the country.

Tom's heart raced as they approached a house. They got down from the horses and knocked on the door. Tom's Aunt Maria answered it.

"Taladon!" she said, drawing him into a hug. "Where have you been?"

"It's a long story," began Taladon. "But Tom's the hero."

"Tom! Elenna! You're safe!" Aunt Maria continued as tears welled up in her eyes. "I'm proud of you both."

Elenna stayed to settle the horses and her grey wolf, Silver, as Tom led the way out to the forge.

"Uncle Henry," he began, opening the door. "There's

someone here to see you."

Henry's mouth gaped wide. "Taladon!" he gasped in surprise. "It's wonderful to have you home."

READ

LEARN TO READ WITH

EARLY READER

 Beast Quest Early Readers are easy-to-read versions of the original books

 Perfect for parents to read aloud and for newly confident readers to read along

 Remember to enjoy reading together. It's never too early to share a story!